THE LITTLE
MATADOR

Words and Pictures by
Julian Hector

Hyperion Books for Children

An Imprint of Disney Book Group

Printed in Singapore
First Edition
1 3 5 7 9 10 8 6 4 2
Library of Congress Cataloging-in-Publication Data on file.
ISBN: 978-1-4231-0779-8
Reinforced binding
Visit www.hyperionbooksforchildren.com

To Mom and Dad

There once lived a Little Matador, who belonged
to a proud family of bullfighters.

Every day, the Little Matador had to practice fighting bulls with his father.

But when his parents weren't watching,
the Little Matador would draw pictures.

He liked drawing animals best,

and they loved to stop and pose for him.

One day, the Little Matador's parents caught him making a scene in the town square. They were very embarrassed.

So the next day they marched him to the
bullring to fight his first bull. "After all, nobody
wants to see a matador draw," they said.

The whole town came to watch.

When the bull came out, he looked very angry,
but the Little Matador refused to fight him.

The bull charged anyway.

As the Little Matador ran, he remembered
what got animals to stop for him.

And it worked!

At first, no one was very excited about this.

But when the crowd saw the finished picture,
they really liked it.

Soon, everyone in town was lining up
to pose for the Little Matador.

That night, the Little Matador's father
called him in for a talk. He had made
an important decision.

And it was the right one.